Pinkalicious

Thanksgiving Helper

HARPER FESTIVAL
An Imprint of HarperCollinsPublishers

by Victoria Kann

To Rebecca,
with many thanks
and much gratitude
—V.K.

The author gratefully acknowledges the
artistic and editorial contributions of
Robert Masheris and Kamilla Benko.

HarperFestival is an imprint of HarperCollins Publishers.

Pinkalicious: Thanksgiving Helper
Copyright © 2014 by Victoria Kann
PINKALICIOUS and all related logos and characters are trademarks of Victoria Kann.
Used with permission.
Based on the HarperCollins book *Pinkalicious*
written by Victoria Kann and Elizabeth Kann, illustrated by Victoria Kann
All rights reserved. Manufactured in China.
No part of this book may be used or reproduced in any manner whatsoever without
written permission except in the case of brief quotations embodied in critical articles and reviews.
For information address HarperCollins Children's Books,
a division of HarperCollins Publishers, 195 Broadway, New York, NY 10007.
www.harpercollinschildrens.com

Library of Congress catalog card number: 2013951714
ISBN 978-0-06-218774-1

Book design by Kirsten Berger
14 15 16 17 18 LEO 10 9 8 7 6 5 4 3 2 1
❖
First Edition

It was Thanksgiving Day! I could hear Mommy baking in the kitchen and could smell the turkey cooking in the oven. Outside, Daddy was raking big piles of leaves.

"Let's go outside," I said to my little brother, Peter.

"Wheee!" we yelled as we jumped into the leaves.

Daddy gave me and Peter rakes. "Why don't you help me?" he asked.

We raked the leaves into more piles.

"Happy Thanksgiviiiing!" I shouted as I leaped into the leaves again.

Peter did a cannonball, yelling, "Gobble gobble gobble!"

"I think that's enough help from you two," Daddy said. "Maybe you can go inside and help your mom."

"Let's pretend it's the first Thanksgiving," I said, putting a pink feather in my hair and a big hat on Peter's head. "You can be Pilgrim Pete, and I will be Princess Pink Feather. This is my wild unicorn, Golden Tail."

"OK!" Peter said. "Now what?"

"Follow me!" I said.

Mommy had decorated the living room and it looked turkeytastic!
Well . . . *almost.* The painting hung crookedly on the wall.
It was too high for us to reach, so I balanced on Golden Tail. . . .

CRUNCH!

Mommy hurried in from the kitchen. "Are you all right? You're not supposed to climb the furniture, Pinkalicious," she said.

I felt terrible. "I'm sorry, Mommy! We were just trying to help."

"Never mind. I'm sure Daddy can fix it," she said. "I need to run to the store. Pinkalicious, Peter, please remind Daddy to check on the turkey while I'm out."

"Maybe there's something we can help Mommy with in the kitchen," I said to Peter. "Follow me!"

I spotted a bag of marshmallows and sweet potatoes ready for mashing. "Look, Pilgrim Pete! Mommy is going to make her Marshmallow-licious Sweet Potato Casserole. Let's help her!"

We looked around for the potato masher but couldn't find it.

"I know!" Peter said. He ran out of the kitchen and came back with the badminton racquets.

"Who knew helping could be so much fun?" I said, as we mashed the potatoes.

Daddy rushed into the kitchen. "Careful," he said. He bent down and picked up the turkey-shaped salt- and pepper shakers. "I think I can fix these."

I slumped. "We are the worst Thanksgiving helpers in the history of Thanksgiving."

"No, you're not. Why don't you set the table while I work on these?"

"Pilgrim Pete, let's set the table so it looks just like the first Thanksgiving," I said. "Do you think they had forks and knives?"

"I can use my arrowhead for a knife," Peter said.

"I know they didn't have light bulbs back then," I said. "We need to find some candles."

"Didn't Native Americans rub rocks together to light a fire?"

"I think so, and they probably used leaves for napkins."

"I bet they used seashells for cups."

"We need corn for the table, too!"

"Pilgrim Pete, do you smell that?" We looked at each other.
"The turkey!"

"Daddy, don't let the turkey burn!" I yelled.

Daddy opened the oven and took out the golden-brown turkey. It was cooked perfectly!

Mommy walked in. "Mmm, the turkey smells good!" she said.

"You can thank Princess Pink Feather and Pilgrim Pete for that!" Daddy said. "They reminded me just in time."

"We also helped set the table," I said. "Come look!"

"We set it so it looks like the first Thanksgiving," Peter said proudly.

Mommy hugged us. "Can I have a feather for my hair, too, Princess Pink Feather?" she asked.

"My fire-starting technique is a little rusty. Mind if I use matches for the candles instead of these rocks?" asked Daddy, as he put on a big hat.

We sat down to eat. Peter tried to pierce his peas with the arrowhead. "I'm thankful for forks," he said.

Daddy laughed. "I'm thankful for matches!"

"I'm thankful we don't have to cook a turkey over an open fire," Mommy said.

"I'm thankful for cups—these seashells don't hold much apple cider," I said. Peter bit into Mommy's decorative corn. "Blech! I'm thankful for rolls!"

"I'm going to miss our Thanksgiving helpers. Do you think Princess Pink Feather and Pilgrim Pete can stick around for a while?" Mommy asked.

I giggled. "We'll see what we can do, but first, please pass the marshmallow sweet potatoes!"